MR WOLF'S PANCAKES

For Mum
and my litter mates:-
Les, Mick, Bren, Keith
Ian ... and Bryn
with love

Jan Fearnley

With very special
thanks to Genevieve
and Ramona.

First published in Great Britain 1999 by Egmont Books
This edition published 2021 by Farshore
An imprint of HarperCollins*Publishers*
1 London Bridge Street, London SE1 9GF
www.farshore.co.uk

HarperCollins*Publishers*
Macken House, 39/40 Mayor Street Upper
Dublin 1, DO1 C9W8
Ireland

Text and illustrations copyright © Jan Fearnley 1999
Jan Fearnley has asserted her moral rights.

ISBN 978 1 4052 8858 3
Printed in the UK by Bell and Bain Ltd, Glasgow
36

A CIP catalogue record for this title is available from the British Library.

MIX
Paper | Supporting
responsible forestry
FSC™ C007454

This book is produced from independently certified FSC™ paper
to ensure responsible forest management.

For more information visit: www.harpercollins.co.uk/green

One day, Mr Wolf was feeling hungry.
He fancied some pancakes.

"Yum, yum!" he said, licking his lips at the
thought of a big pile of fresh, delicious pancakes.

Mr Wolf had never made pancakes before,
so he took his big recipe book down off the shelf
and looked inside.

But wolves can't read very well and Mr Wolf
had trouble making sense of it. So he went to get
some help from his neighbours.

He called on Chicken Licken who lived nearby.

"Please can you help me read this?" he asked.

"No!" said Chicken Licken, slamming
the door in Mr Wolf's face – **BANG!**

"Oh, dear," sighed Mr Wolf.
He sat down, slowly read the book,
and worked out what he needed – all by himself.

Mr Wolf looked in his cupboard for the ingredients,
but he couldn't find anything he needed.

"I'll go to the shop," he decided,
and he settled down to write a list.

But wolves aren't very good at writing,
so Mr Wolf called on Wee Willy Winky.

"You're very clever,"
said Mr Wolf. "Can you help me
write my shopping list, please?"
"No!" said Wee Willy Winky. "Go away!"
He slammed his door – **BANG!**

"There's no need to be like that,"
said Mr Wolf quietly.

Mr Wolf sat down and tried very hard with his writing
until he had made his shopping list – all by himself.

Now he needed to count his money
to make sure he had enough.

But wolves aren't very good at counting,
so he went to the Gingerbread Man for some help.

"Can you help me count my money, please?" he asked politely.
"No! I'm too busy to bother with you!"
said the Gingerbread Man, slamming his door – **BANG!**

So poor Mr Wolf had to sit down and count his money.
It took him a long time and he had to check it
three times before it was right.
But he did it – all by himself.

Mr Wolf needed a basket to carry his shopping,
so he called on Little Red Riding Hood.

"Please may I borrow your basket?"
he asked very nicely.
"I'm not lending my basket to you!"
said Little Red Riding Hood. "Now, clear off!"

So Mr Wolf set off to the shop
without a basket.
"I'll manage," he said.

Mr Wolf went to the shop.

He looked at his list, remembered what
he needed, counted out his money, and carried
the eggs, milk and flour home – all by himself.

Now it was time to make the pancakes.
But wolves aren't very good at cooking,
so Mr Wolf called on the Three Little Pigs.

"Please can you help me cook my pancakes?
I'll share them with you," he said kindly.

"No chance!" chorused the pigs,
slamming their doors –
BANG! BANG! BANG!

Mr Wolf felt sad because nobody
wanted to help him.

Mr Wolf went home and started
to make the pancakes – all by himself.
Soon there was a huge pile of delicious
pancakes on the table, all ready for eating.

Now, as Mr Wolf had been making his pancakes, a lovely
smell had drifted out of the kitchen. All his neighbours
could smell it and it made them feel very hungry.

They wanted some pancakes too.
They decided to try their luck.

So, they knocked on Mr Wolf's door.
"Give us some of your pancakes!" said the rotten lot.
"Why should I give any to you?" said Mr Wolf.
"Not one of you would help me."
"We'll help you eat them," replied Mr Wolf's
neighbours nastily. "Anyway, we're not going
away until you give us some!"

Mr Wolf thought very hard for a moment.
There was only one decent thing to do.

"Oh, very well then," he sighed,
"you had better come in."

Mr Wolf opened the door wide and whoosh!
His greedy neighbours rudely pushed him aside
and dashed down the hall.

Mr Wolf shook his head, shrugged his
shoulders, followed them into the kitchen
and when they were all in . . .

Mr Wolf gobbled them up.

SNIPPITY!

SNAPPITY!

That was the end of his unhelpful neighbours!

And then, with his bulging tummy not quite full,
Mr Wolf sat down to eat his pile of pancakes –
and he did it all by himself.

Well, there was nobody else around.